"This well told story of good and evil, anchored in the historical violence of Serbia in the late twentieth century, is nothing short of spellbinding!"

—AMANDA HANNA
Novelist and International Political Ghostwriter

"Ray Lopez writes with the kind of clarity and conviction that comes from a life genuinely crafted by what he believes. *The Second Coming of Joan* is rooted in his Christianity, yet it's also surprisingly accessible and deeply human in its reach. I appreciated how Lopez invites the reader into spiritual reflection without losing the power of the story. His prose expresses strength, purpose, and a moral faith that feels less like being preached at and more like being called toward courage and a belief that will pull you through the storm. Whether you share his faith or simply value writing that aims the heart towards hope and understanding, this is a book worth spending time with. Ray Lopez has a distinctive voice, and *The Second Coming of Joan* delivers a message that lingers."

—EDDIE K. WRIGHT
Author of *Gangster Turned Guru Presents: A day in the Life of Coffee and Paradise*

"In his latest novel, *The Second Coming of Joan*, Ray Lopez delivers a moving portrait of a young girl, Nadja. Through her eyes, the reader experiences the many horrors of war as her family makes their escape from Sarajevo, Bosnia, to a Red Cross refugee camp. As the story unfolds, we find that Nadja and her family do not drudge this perilous road alone. This book is a page turner!"

—WARREN MAXWELL
Author and Historian

"Ray Lopez's novel, *The Second Coming of Joan*, compellingly invites the reader to witness firsthand the vileness and destruction of war through the eyes of a young Serbian girl as she, her mother, and younger brother flee their home in Sarajevo to a refugee camp in Croatia, and eventually to a better life in the Netherlands. The magic of this tale lies in the author's ability to interweave Nadja's innermost thoughts as she experiences unspeakable horrors and struggles to understand her place within the ever-changing landscape of the war with the parallel story of Joan of Arc and the search for spiritual comfort and meaning in this dark and dangerous world. A truly beautiful tale of survival, discovering your light, and ultimately hope. I highly recommend it."

—DAVID ADAM GILL
Published Playwright, Teacher,
and Co-founder, New Ambassadors Theatre Company

The Second Coming of Joan

The Second Coming of Joan

By Ray Lopez

RESOURCE *Publications* • Eugene, Oregon

THE SECOND COMING OF JOAN

Resource Publications
An Imprint of Wipf and Stock Publishers
199 W. 8th Ave., Suite 3
Eugene, OR 97401

www.wipfandstock.com

PAPERBACK ISBN: 978-1-6667-8937-9
HARDCOVER ISBN: 978-1-6667-8938-6
EBOOK ISBN: 978-1-6667-8939-3

VERSION NUMBER 032426

Cover Art by Hilary Houseman Goduti
Illustrations by Tebben Gill Lopez

Dedicated to Nadija Ferizovic

March 11, 1953—August 6, 2022

Preface

The Socialist Federal Republic of Yugoslavia, founded in 1943 during World War II, was a federation made up of six republics: Slovenia, Croatia, Bosnia-Herzegovina, Serbia, Montenegro and Macedonia. It was ruled by Marshal Josip Tito following the end of World War II with Muslims, Catholics, and Orthodox citizens living cohesively.

Between 1992 and 1995, an inhumane plan was executed to ethnically cleanse Bosnia with the planned, systematic, and industrialized killings of non-Serbs, the majority being Bosniak-Muslims.

Following Tito's death in 1980, ethnic-nationalism began to rise. In 1991, the country began to disintegrate along ethnic lines. Slovenia and Croatia declared their independence in June 1991, prompting war. As the rise of Greater Serb expansions began to gain traction in February of 1992 a referendum on independence was held in Bosnia-Herzegovina (BiH) and 99.7% of voters voted yes.

The Bosnian Serb leadership boycotted the referendum to prevent independence, but independence was officially declared on 1 March 1992 and internationally recognized by April 1992. The Siege of Sarajevo resulted in over 11,000 people killed, of which 1,600 were just children.

Between 1992–95, the citizens of Sarajevo were subjected to daily shelling and sniper attacks, cut off from the rest of the world.

Shortly after the referendum, Serb forces seized the city of Sarajevo which would lead to a 4 year-long campaign of terror and persecution. From May 1992, Bosnian-Serb Forces under the command of General Ratko Mladić used shelling and sniping to target civilian areas of the city and key institutions, killing, wounding, and inflicting terror upon the civilian population. During this time, almost all of Sarajevo's cultural, religious, and residential buildings were either partially or completely destroyed.

From January to March 1993, the Bosnian-Serb Forces attacked the Cerska area in eastern BiH. Thousands of Muslims fled to the UN 'Safe Areas' of Srebrenica and Žepa in hopes of finding safety. Thereafter, Bosnian Serb Forces began to focus particular attention on capturing the strategically located Srebrenica and Žepa enclave and expelling the Bosnian Muslim population that had fled there in the wake of the 1992 and 1993 "ethnic cleansing" campaigns in eastern Bosnia-Herzegovina.

On March 8, 1995, Radovan Karadžić (the political leader of the Bosnian-Serbs), ordered the Serb Forces to eliminate the Muslim enclaves of Srebrenica and Žepa, escalating the "strategic objectives" of May 12, 1992. On July 2, 1995, Bosnian Serb Forces attacked the Srebrenica enclave.

This attack continued until July 11, 1995, when Ratko Mladić and the Bosnian Serb Forces entered Srebrenica. Subsequently, those forces terrorized Bosnian Muslims, who were forcibly transferred to areas outside the enclave and many of whom fled in a huge column through the woods towards Tuzla (a free territory). The vast majority of this group consisted of civilians. Nearly 8,000 Bosnian Muslim prisoners captured in the area around Srebrenica were summarily executed from July 13 to July 19, 1995.

The Bosnian war and genocide resulted in close to 100,000 civilians killed, over 2 million people forcibly displaced, and between 20,000–50,000 women systematically raped. All due to their ethnic and religious identity.

Joan of Arc was a French peasant girl who, during the Hundred Years' War, claimed divine guidance to lead the French army to victory. A national heroine of France, she was captured and executed by the English at age 19 but later canonized as a saint.

Acknowledgments

I must start by thanking Christ for saving my life, blessing me with my wife, and the experiences he has brought me through which have given me something to write about. I thank my wife, Paula, for loving me, regardless, and forever being my number one reader. I am grateful for my other readers and supporters. I am thankful for my daughter, the artist Tebben, for keeping me on point and directing me to keep Joan in the story, also for her amazing illustrations of Joan in battle against the demons, Slubgoeb and Glubuse! I am thankful for my big sister, Teresa Haft, who said it was a good read and reassured me, when I asked about the rape scenes, that they were an integral part of the journey. I am very grateful for my primary reader, and editor, David Adam Gill, award winning published playwright. Thank you for the time you put into this book and for teaching me how to write strong, purposeful dialogue. I am also grateful for the artist, Hilary Houseman Goduti, whose reading inspired her wonderful cover art. I am so thankful for the careful reading, early suggestions and encouragement of Amanda Hanna, Amazon Best Selling Novelist & International Political Ghost Writer. Finally, I am grateful for the inspiration I received from reading the novel *Joan of Arc* by Mark Twain, the play *Saint Joan* by George Bernard Shaw, and *The Screwtape Letters* by C.S. Lewis.

Chapter One

Nadja didn't know she was Muslim until the war started. There was no religion before that. But she was 8-years old and very smart, a Straight A student. Math and Science were her favorite subjects, and she was on the gymnastics club. She learned quickly what religion was and what it meant to be Muslim. It was hate and meant people wanted to hurt you, and you had to hide and be afraid. But she was happy before that.

It was springtime in Sarajevo, Bosnia, 1992, and she lived in a three-bedroom apartment with her parents, her younger brother, Danir, and her little shih tzu dog, Whiskers. She was waiting, excitedly, to go to her best friend, Amelia's house for a birthday party! She was imagining the joy on Amelia's face after she opened her gift, a Barbie Doll. She held the Barbie up and looked in the mirror. People always said that she looked like her mother. She had creamy white skin, reddish brown hair and dark brown eyes.

She looked away and was showing the Barbie to Whiskers, when her parents burst into her room! She saw her father holding Danir, closely to his chest, and he had a large black duffel bag strapped around his shoulders. Whiskers began barking and jumping around, while her father pulled her to her feet and she followed her parents through the bedroom door, and out of the apartment. Nadja dropped the doll, picked up Whiskers, held him tightly to her chest, and asked her mother, her majka, Irma, "What's happening!?"

"Nadja!" shouted Irma, "There's no time to explain. We must go, now!"

In the lobby on the first floor, people were running back and forth. Nadja heard sirens and a soft pounding noise in the background, like bursts of thunder in the distance. She saw her neighbors racing from the building, carrying suitcases in one hand and pulling their children with the other. There was so much noise circling around them. Her father put Danir down and said, "Nadja, take care of your brother."

Everything had changed when her parents brought Danir home from the hospital. In fact, things started changing before that. They said he came too soon from her mother's belly, and he was small and sick. He couldn't breathe on his own and was living in a tube at the hospital. Her father was at his toy factory most of the time, much more than before Danir was born. And her majka was at the hospital with Danir almost all the time. Fortunately, she got to stay with her maternal grandma, her baka, Pamba, whom she loved so much, especially when she called her princess.

When her brother came home, he took up most of her mother's time. Irma was a psychologist before Danir was born, working with adolescents from alcoholic homes. Nadja was with her grandma when her mom was at work, but they made dinner together after she came home, and she played dolls with Nadja after, read her stories at bedtime and sang her to sleep. Now, her mom was on a sabbatical and was home. But she had to be with Danir. She had to use a nebulizer three times a day and massage his tiny arms and legs because the doctors said he wouldn't be able to walk. She didn't listen to them. She told Nadja she had to be a big girl, a good big sister and help with her little brother, but she just seemed to get in the way. Her mother started giving her cake and ice cream as rewards for being good and Nadja started gaining weight.

After Danir grew stronger, they began leaving the house together and going to the park. He was crawling and trying to pull himself up. The doctors said it was a miracle. Once he was walking, her mother began to pay more attention to her. She told her she had gained a little too much weight, and she was going to put her in ballet.

When Nadja went to her first class she was embarrassed. All the other girls were skinny; and she was the only one wearing a pink tutu. The rest of the girls wore white. They looked at her and whispered and giggled. She didn't want to go back.

Nadia saw her parents facing each other; they were crying, and all sound stopped but for their words,

"My love, I have to go."

"I know," said her mother as she buried her face in her father's chest and began sobbing and breathing in deeply. And for Nadja, there was nothing but her parents, Danir, and Whiskers. The others were a blur of soundless motion when her mother said to her father, "Just go." He knelt before them and hugged her and Danir harder than she could ever remember. He pulled back and said, "Nadja, I must go and fight for Bosnia. Take care of your mother and Danir." He handed the duffel bag to Irma and was gone, out with the rushing crowd.

Danir was crying. They were standing in the middle of the lobby. Nadja saw that there were fewer people running around and could hear the sirens and soft pounding again. Her mother knelt and wrapped her arms around Nadja and Danir. Whiskers scrambled around their feet and was barking, barking, barking.

"We have to go into the basement."

"Mama, I'm scared. Why are we going down there?"

Danir was crying louder now.

"Nadja listen to me. It will be alright. It's only for short while."

Danir kept crying.

"Mama! Where did Papa go?"

"With the army. There is a war."

"What? What war?"

"Nadja! Just listen to me. We must go into the basement now! We must hide."

"From who?"

Irma took each of her children by the hand and started leading them to the door that opened to a stairwell taking them down to the basement. Whiskers followed close behind. Irma opened the door and paused to look around before they entered. The last thing Nadja saw before descending was her friend, Victor, and his father heading for the front of the building. She and Victor caught the fear in each other's eyes.

Chapter Two

They had been in the basement for weeks, living off dry goods and canned food. It was cold, dark, and smelled of mold, oil, and ashes. The shelling had destroyed the upper floors of the building and there were a few other families hiding as well, each in their own space. There was a sink in the laundry room with running water, but they had run out of food and were very hungry. Nadja's stomach was a big knot, and she couldn't sleep. The sirens were constant and the pounding was getting louder. Her mom was cooking something over the fire, under an open window, a small animal. Danir was warming himself near the fire and Irma just stared into the flames.

Nadja hadn't seen Whiskers all day and decided to search for him before they ate. She moved around the dark basement, the familiar hallways, storage rooms and open spaces. The other families were all gone. They had gone out looking for food and not returned. It was dirty and she could see the dust stirring in the air as she searched. There were only a few small windows letting in the dimming light of the fall dusk and the sound of sirens and the pounding bombs getting louder and closer.

"Whiskers, where are you?!"

A bomb exploded a little closer; the building shook and dirt fell from the ceiling. Irma called from the distance,

"Nadja, what are you doing?"

"Majka, I have to find Whiskers."

"Forget about that dog and come and eat!"

Nadja continued to search for Whiskers, ignoring her mother. She passed by storage rooms she was familiar with then stopped in front of the room, with the Caution/Furnace sign on the door, that she had never entered. She saw that the door was open. She could still hear her mother calling in the background.

"Nadja! Where are you girl!"

She heard her mother's voice getting closer.

"Nadja!"

She entered the room and strained to see in the dying light. There was a small light bulb hanging down. Nadja pulled the cord, the bulb flickered, then stayed lit, offering a small amount of light for her to see. Her mother's voice was growing louder and angrier.

"Nadija! Answer me right now!"

Nadja whispered for her dog, "Whiskers?"

"Nadja! Where are you!"

The room was cold. It was hard to see. She looked in the shadows, behind the dark furnace. Her mother's voice was closer.

"Nadja! Answer me!"

She found a square door in the wall behind the furnace, about 2'by2', with a small wooden handle. She slowly opened it and reached her hand into the darkness. She felt the cold brick and pulled back from the spiderwebs. She wiped the webs from her hand, took a deep breath and reached in again, a little further this time, and touched, what felt like, a wooden box. Her mother's voice faded away as she reached in with both hands and retrieved the box. It was difficult to see in the small light, but Nadja brushed away the dust to see the box was made of reddish wood with a golden clasp in front. She opened it to find four books inside. She pulled out a Quran and a Bible. They were large, and leatherbound. She had never seen them before and had no idea what they were about. The third book she found was a bound manuscript titled, *The Islamic Declaration*. Nadja remembered hearing people talking about this book, and the author, on the news. But she was deeply drawn to the last book. The title was *Joan of Arc*, by Mark Twain and there was an illustration on the cover of a beautiful young woman atop a white stallion, wearing silver armor and holding a sword. She placed the other books back in the box, picked up the book of Joan, and held it up, towards the light, with both hands, captivated by the image when her mother charged into the room.

"Nadja!"

Irma grabbed her by the arm.

"What are you doing in here!? Why didn't you answer me?!"

She saw the book Nadja was holding, then saw the books in the box.

"Oh my god! How did you find these!?"

Nadja saw that her mother was frightened and started crying.

"I'm sorry mama. I was looking for Whiskers. I know I'm not supposed to come into this room, but the door was open."

Irma quickly grabbed the box, pulled Nadja to her feet and dragged her from the room. She clutched the Joan of Arc book to her chest as her mother pulled her to the other end of the basement.

"We must eat! And then we must burn these books; and go to sleep. Your brother is already sleeping. He is very tired so stop that crying!"

"But I have to find Whiskers, mama."

"Be quiet about that dog! Be quiet! Not another word!"

They arrived at the far corner of the basement where the fire still burned under a spit with the small headless animal, still roasting. Danir was sound asleep near the fire.

"Don't wake up your brother. We must eat quickly."

Nadja suddenly remembered how hungry she was and sat down near the fire, still clutching the book to her chest. She watched her mother pull small pieces of flesh from the animal and place them on a plate for her. She took the plate and began to eat, ravenously. It tasted strange to her, and had a dark, greasy texture.

"Slow down. Don't eat so fast. Remember to chew your food. Here, have some water."

Irma gave Nadja a jar of water and removed the rest of the animal from the spit. She placed the books on the fire, then looked at her daughter who finished the portion of meat on her plate, eating with one hand, still holding the book.

They stared at each other with their "listening eyes" and time stood still.

"You can have the book my love, but you must keep it hidden, always."

Nadja started to breathe again. Irma placed a few more small pieces of meat on Nadja's plate and began pulling off the rest and placing it on a sheet of aluminum foil.

"Eat slowly and have some more water."

"What about Whiskers mama?"

"Eat the rest of your meat.

Nadja placed a piece of meat in her mouth and savored the warmth and taste before she swallowed.

"Mama. What happened to Whiskers? Where is he?"

"I'm sorry my love. Whiskers is gone."

Chapter Three

After that meal they started leaving the building in search of food. Irma had strict rules about these trips. Nadja was to hold on to the hem of her coat and keep her eyes on her mother's back. She was never to look away. Danir held onto Nadja's hand with the same instruction.

But it was impossible. There was too much to see. Too many people, mothers and children, and broken bodies on the ground, and the blood, and the crying, and the screaming, and the silence. Some of the bodies reminded Nadja of their last meal in the basement, charred. She always kept her book with her. She even slept with it under her jacket. When they walked through the carnage, she pressed it closer to her heart.

She had been reading about Joan, this young woman who prayed to God and spoke with three saints, Catherine, Margaret, and Michael, who came down from heaven and gave her instructions from God. Joan prayed all the time, every day, and God answered her prayers. He gave her strength, knowledge, and great courage to lead the French army into battle and victory. And she was only a peasant girl. She couldn't even read. Nadja was amazed by this true story. She consumed it. It gave her strength. She wanted to be like Joan.

Nadja wanted to talk to her mother about the book, but she was afraid. She remembered how she burned the other books. She remembered her mother telling her that the Quran and the

Bible were about God, that there was no God, and she was never to speak about it again. But Joan believed in God and Nadja wanted to believe. So, she started to think about praying but didn't know how.

Irma was very excited that cold winter morning as she bundled her children up in their coats and scarves.

"The Red Cross has opened a station just outside the city!" she said.

"What is the Red Cross Mama?" asked Nadia.

"It's a place where there is food and water, and doctors and nurses for the people."

The moment she heard the words food and water, Nadja again remembered how hungry she was, how the pain in her stomach was constant, how it kept her awake at night.

And her fear was constant. She could also see it in her mother's eyes, feel it in her arms when she hugged her and held her hand. But, when they went outside, she was never able to follow the rules. She held on to her mother's coat and tried to keep her eyes straight ahead. She had seen the destruction left by the bombs, the burned and broken buildings and bodies on the street. She knew that when the sirens sounded there would be more. And she learned who the enemy was, the Serbs, some Bosnian, and others, invading soldiers. It was all the mothers spoke about, how they were getting closer, how they had to get out of the city, but where would they go? But today felt different, they were going to the Red Cross where they would be safe!

Nadja always looked at their car when they left the building. It was blackened, by the bombs, with broken windows and melted tires. They walked through the streets covered with mud and snow. It was a long way and there were many other women and children, more than Nadja had seen any other time they left the basement. It was hard. Nadja's feet became heavy, and it felt like the snow and mud were trying to suck her into the ground. Irma never looked back. She just kept walking with the crowd. Nadja held onto her mother's coat and her brother's hand. Danir just kept crying. He cried all the time now, except when he fell asleep.

After what seemed like the longest walk of Nadja's life, they were outside the city, traveling on a road surrounded by trees. It looked familiar and she remembered her life before the war. This was the road they would drive on when they went to the cottage by the lake for the summer. But now it was snowing.

"Nadja, we're almost there!" Irma said, "We're almost there! Just over that hill up ahead. Do you see it Nadja? Are you still holding your brother's hand? Danir, stop crying now. We're almost. . ."

The sirens roared again and sounded louder outside the city. They had never ventured far from the basement and had always sheltered within minutes of the sound. The moving mass of people stopped. Screams rose in concert with sirens. Some started to run ahead, others turned back, and others, like Nadja, her mother and brother, stood still and looked up. Nadja watched the snowflakes coming down. She tried to catch them on her tongue. The clouds began to roar as the dark jets soared above, one, two, three. . .the thunderous explosion lit up the sky beyond the hill. Nadja was blinded by the light but held onto her mother's coat, and her brother's hand, as they were pushed to the ground by a rushing hot wind.

Nadja was lying on a lounge chair on the cottage deck overlooking the lake. The sun sparkling on the water was so bright. She looked up at the blinding white light and felt a slight drizzle of rain falling on her face, but it was hard, like little pebbles and there were sirens.

"Nadja, my love: are you okay? Nadja, wake up. Nadja, get up!"

Nadja sat upright and breathed in smoke. Her mother was holding crying Danir. Irma wrapped her arms around her children and sobbed deeply, while Nadja began coughing. It was like they were in a cloud. It was still snowing but there was also ash falling down. The sirens were blaring, muffled by the ringing in Nadja's ears, and everyone was running back towards the city. For Nadja it felt like slow motion like when she tried to run underwater at the lake, and all the noise sounded far away like when she wore her earmuffs, and there was a ringing. Then they were up, her mother holding crying Danir, grabbed Nadja's hand, and they were running.

Now, they never left the basement and there was no water. They huddled together in a corner farthest from the stairs. There were no more sirens, no more bombs, but new sounds outside, like the firecrackers her grandfather would light at the lake cottage during warm, summer nights when Nadja would catch fireflies and put them in a glass jar. But these sounds were different, they were deeper and there was a rhythm, like rat tat tat tat. The Serbs had entered the city. They were searching the buildings. Irma told them they had to be quiet as a mouse. Danir was no longer crying; he mostly slept.

They heard footsteps approaching. Irma looked at Nadja and held her pointer finger to her lips. Nadja knew to be quiet and tried to hold her breath but when she saw her friend Victor and his father approaching, she was so happy they had come to help and cried out "Victor!" in her joy. "No Nadj," whispered Irma as she reached to place her hand over Nadja's mouth. Then three soldiers stepped out of the shadows and came towards them. They looked massive to Nadja, dressed in black, wearing helmets, they had guns, and their faces were covered with black bandanas. Her friend Victor and his father disappeared. Irma screamed and Danir started crying. Irma stood up with her children and pushed them behind her. One of the soldiers slapped her to the ground, grabbed her by the hair and pulled her forward while the other two each grabbed Nadja and Danir over their shoulders and carried them away, kicking and crying, over their shoulders like sacks of screaming chaos.

Chapter Four

Nadja started praying after they were put in the cage. She prayed that her papa was safe and would come to rescue them. And one of her prayers had already been answered. The soldiers let the mothers stay with their children, but there were so many and so little room. The cage was a twenty-foot square. Nadja counted it out, even though it was so crowded, by walking heel to toe, like she learned in ballet class for balance, going from corner to corner.

Once a day, the guards would bring them stale bread and dish out a cold brown mush from a bucket into bowls for them to eat. In a corner opposite from the gate there was a large pot, with large ring handles, where people would pee and poop. It smelled horrible. The soldiers would only empty it when it overflowed. Two of the mothers would carry it out to be emptied and cleaned, which felt like a very long time, at least an hour, or what Nadja thought was an hour. She tried to measure time by counting to sixty, sixty times, but would always lose count along the way. Sometimes some of the children had to go so bad that they couldn't hold it and soiled themselves. This happened to Danir many times, but not Nadja.

She hardly ever had to go but was always thirsty. Like the poop pot, the soldiers provided the same size pot, filled with water, with a large ladle hanging from a chain. They would refill it once it was empty. The women would be forced to carry this as well, and it would also take at least an hour, as far as Nadja could count, before they returned. Sometimes they would take out both pots at the same time and Nadja always wondered if they switched them, which made her less thirsty.

When the women returned, they were very quiet for a very long time. They would often go to a corner and curl up into a ball, like a baby, and go to sleep. The other women would look away. It always became very quiet during those times. It seemed that Nadja's mother was always chosen to go with the soldiers. But she was stronger than the other mothers. When she came back she wouldn't curl up in a ball and sleep; she would hug Nadja and Danir, and kiss them, and kiss them, and kiss them.

Nadja didn't know how, but she continued to pray. Like what she read about Joan, she just prayed from her heart. She still had the book. She kept it hidden under her clothes the whole time. She prayed that Jesus, who had suffered for her sins, would bring them to a better place.

And in heaven God listened. He called to Michael and said, "*I have not heard prayers such as these for over six hundred years, not since the songs sung by my sweet Joan. They are fearless, born simply through faith and imagination. They will bring healing to my heart which will be pierced by the same nails from Calvary, eight thousand times, from all those to be slaughtered and lost in Srebrenica.*

"Lord, you feel the suffering from events yet to come." said Michael.

"Always," replied the Lord, "But this terror will birth great love in many who will overcome this great evil with good."

Then Nadja saw God answer her prayers again. Her mama was beautiful, and she always noticed how people treated her, with smiles and kindness, especially her papa, and other men they would meet or pass by. She remembered how her papa would hug and kiss her mama and tell her how beautiful she was. She thought about it when the soldiers came one day and took them to a smaller cage in a different part of the camp. It was in a building that looked and smelled like the basement where they had lived. The cage was half the size, but they were alone, just Nadja, her mother and brother, and there was a bed the three of them shared. There was a lightbulb hanging down from the ceiling which helped Nadja to read. There were other cages in the building, but it was dark and there were black curtains separating them. They couldn't see, but they could hear each other. The soldiers came that first day and took Irma.

And God called to the angel, "Michael. Come to me now."

And Michael appeared and said, "Yes Lord; how can I serve?"

"These prayers from this child, Nadja, are precious and powerful."

"Yes Lord. I see. I can hear them now."

"We have not heard such prayers since the songs of Joan. I will change her into a new creation, a new being, and I will send her down to the realm below and she will lead your army, like she did as a child on earth. Go to the Hall of Worship and bring her. This time she will rise from the flames!"

Chapter Five

When the soldiers came, Irma would go quietly. She didn't want to frighten her children. Sometimes there were one, two, or even three, and it would happen at any time of the day or night. She would tell Nadja, "Don't be frightened. I won't be far away." Nadja knew this was true, because she could hear them behind the black curtain. He mother would say, "Play with your brother. Tell him stories about your Joan of Arc." She had been talking with Nadja about what she was reading and learning about the heroic feats of the peasant girl. She had always thought of the story as a romantic fantasy created by the Catholic church. But she was starting to understand it as so much more, and it gave her hope for her daughter, as she saw her finding peace and comfort from the book.

The worst times were when the soldiers were drunk. Nadja tried to be brave, but she couldn't help being afraid. She saw the look in their eyes. Sometimes they were bloodshot, sometimes big and large, but there was always a look of hunger and excitement, like her dog, when he was about to eat.

They were sleeping when the light came on and two soldiers stumbled into the cage. They were drinking from a bottle. Nadja knew they were drunk and could harm her mother, so she grabbed Irma around her waist and began to cry out, "No! Leave her alone! Go away and leave us alone!"

Danir started crying. It was always the same, like a play being acted again, and again, and again. One of the soldiers pulled her away, threw her to the floor, and said, "Shut up you little bitch of a whore or we won't bring her back this time! And stop your crying!"

And they took Irma behind the black curtain. And the entire time, she would listen to her children cry; it gave her comfort; she knew they were there. Otherwise, she would be lost.

And Nadja tried to be brave for her mother and Danir. She stopped crying and started singing the songs her Baka Pamba taught her when she was a little girl, before the war. She tried to drown out the sounds of the struggle, but she had to listen. She heard the soldiers laughing, and grunting. But she couldn't hear her mother and started to pray. "Dear God. Protect my mama. Don't let them hurt her. Make them stop. Bring her back to us again." Then Nadja heard the soldiers yelling and clapping and heard her mother crying softly. Nadja was sobbing and trembling and Danir was crying again. The soldiers became louder, the grunting, and there were other voices and grunting and cheering, all together. And Nadja tried to continue her prayer, while crying, sobbing, and holding Damir, "God, please . . . ." She was kneeling in the center of the cage, holding her brother when she heard a sound, like thunder, but continued to pray, "God make me brave like Joan of Arc. . ." while crying, sobbing, and rocking back and forth with Danir. "Give me her strength."

She felt a soft, warm breeze flow through the cage as Joan appeared and touched her on the top of her head. Nadja's entire body tingled, as she felt a warmth spread through her and felt like crying and laughing at once. She turned and froze, unable to speak or move. Then Joan said her name, "*Nadja.*"

It was the sweetest sound she had ever heard.

"Nadja, it is alright. They cannot hurt you. Your mama will soon be with you. Look up and see me my child."

Nadja slowly raised her eyes. Joan was dressed in a long brown gown with a sleeveless tunic of the same color. Her reddish-brown hair was shortly cropped above her ears and there was a golden aura around her.

"Who are you?" she asked as she looked to see that the gate was still locked.

"How did you get here?"

"Through your prayers." answered Joan.

"My prayers? How. . .?"

"He heard you, and I am here. We are not meant to understand."

But who are you?

"I am Joan, Joan of Arc. Some called me The Maid. You've been praying about me, or so I been told."

"Where's your armor and your sword?"

"I do not need them today. No worries child. For God says, 'The secret things belong to the Lord our God, but the things revealed belong to us and our children forever,'"

"Revealed?"

"All I know this moment is I was sent to help you. The Father heard your prayers and decided he needed to do something new. For I was a saint in heaven. All I had to do was worship. I was with my family, and friends, and there were other saints, and it was beautiful, all the time."

"Then what happened? God heard my prayers and sent you?"

"Yes. During the middle of worship, the angel, Michael, appeared by my side and said, 'You must come with me.'"

"And where did he bring you?"

"I do not know exactly, I suppose the angel hall of heaven. And when I arrived, I saw other angels, some who I recognized, like Barbiel and Gabriel."

"How do you know them?"

"Well, they would show up to worship sometimes. Barbiel once explained that the angels must lead worship on a rotation since Lucifer was cast down."

"Lucifer?"

"Yes. He led all worship before. There was a battle because he wanted to be like God. There was division between the angels. Michael led the way and Lucifer and his followers were defeated and fell to earth."

"I don't understand. How are you going to help us?"

"This is what I have learned. When I got to the angel place, they were all talking, loudly, Michael and Gabriel and some others I didn't know. They sounded like they were arguing and did not notice me at all. Michael looked at me, shrugged his wings, and walked to the group to point me out."

"What did they tell you?"

"Well, nothing at first. They just kept on talking like I was not there!"

"What were they saying?"

"Well, Michael was saying that this has never happened before. A saint has never been sent into battle. Gabriel agreed with him and said, 'And a female saint, at that!'"

At that moment a loud explosion rocked the building, causing the hanging lightbulb to sway back and forth.

"Our time is precious. I shall finish telling you what I learned. First, it is true that a saint in heaven has never been sent to Earth to engage in warfare. It has always been the task of angels, and all the angels have been male. I wasn't surprised to hear that after what I experienced during my life on earth."

"I know. I read about you in this book I found. It has a picture of you on the cover on a white horse, wearing silver armor and holding up a sword."

"Yes, that was me. So, the angels went on about how no saint ever returned to Earth, which I would not know, because I was never able to read the scriptures. But before I was sent, Michael took me aside and explained that God can change things as he pleases, that he heard your prayers and decided that he needed to do a new thing and he remolded me into a saint and an angel, reminding Michael how I was made in his, God's own, image, higher than an angel and now I'm here!"

"And, what happens now?" asked Nadja.

"Michael said that you and I will work together, to keep you and your mother and brother safe and help others as well."

"And, how are we going to do that?"

"He said that we would learn along the way, and he will also be guiding us, revealing special instructions when needed."

They paused and remained still for a moment. Nadja noticed that the yellow aura around Joan was intensifying."

"Do you hear that?" Joan asked. There was silence and Nadja noticed that Danir was asleep in her arms.

"I don't hear a thing. Is my mama okay? Is she coming back?"

"Listen with your heart and you will hear that her healing has begun."

Nadja strained to hear but could not and Joan saw the frustration on her face.

"Nadja, be still and listen."

And she was and thought she heard something like the wind,

"Still. . ."

then faint voices,

"Listen. . ."

Then singing, the most beautiful chorus she had ever heard.

And her face became bathed in the golden aura that now extended from Joan.

"I hear it. It's beautiful."

"It is the angels and saints in heaven rejoicing in this battle won today. I must go now. Your mama is coming soon."

"Why? Why can't you stay?!"

"No worries. I am here now in the realm between heaven and earth. You will not always see me but know that I am here. And I can see that you believe in your heart, that God raised his son from the grave. And he wants to fill you with the gift of the Holy Spirit now if you confess with your mouth that Christ is Lord. Do you confess that now, Nadja?"

"Yes."

"Then breathe in deeply now the Holy Spirit of God."

And together they breathed in through their noses and out through their mouths, and Nadja felt a peace she couldn't understand.

"No worries my sweet Nadja. Your dreams will be filled with visions of the glory to be. Your mama is here now, and you are strong and brave. I will return."

At that moment, Nadja felt a soft, warm breeze flow through her body, as she turned towards the gate and heard the soldiers approaching with her mama. She turned back for a moment, and Joan was gone.

Chapter Six

In the spiritual realm above Sarajevo, Joan was about to engage in battle with Slubgoeb, a demon who oversaw sexual assault, specifically rape. He was mostly a large, shrouded shadow, a red eyed, shape shifting creature, who would appear as a large primate, a hairy man, or caught halfway between the two.

When they came for her that morning, Irma looked at Nadja with all her strength. Danir had already crawled under the bed.

"Nadja, sing to your brother, read to him. Be strong like your Joan."

"Yes mama," Nadja replied while wiping away her tears and trying not to cry. As the two guards lifted Irma to her feet, she kept eye contact with Nadja and prepared to be taken, again. Whether it was her daughter's cries, or her voice struggling to sing, Irma stayed focused on her children, which would eventually take her to a higher place.

This time, she couldn't ignore the pain to her body and heart. She screamed and began to cry.

Slubgoeb drew strength from her anguish,

"This is going so well. The guards are heeding my call. And some are now doing it on their own. I don't even need to whisper."

Whenever Irma became vocal it would excite the guards. Slubgoeb could feel their pleasure, licking his lips, *"Mmmm. It is time to play with hearts and souls. And the day has just begun!"*

The sounds filled the air, heightening Slubgoeb's arousal which he poured into the guards.

"Yes. This is going to be delicious!" he thrilled.

A rhythm emerged between shouts and cries, and Slubgoeb rejoiced,

"Oh, the music! The beat, the beauty!"

Irma's cries rose and peaked the demon's joy, *"Ahhh. There it is. The voice of an angel being tortured."*

The guard's voice rose in time with Irma's cries, *"And there it is again, the beautiful duet I am known to compose. It is glorious!"*

Slubgoeb began waving his arms, conducting his new symphony *"It is triumphant!"*

Captain Petrovic entered the cell and commanded the guards to "Stop!"

"No! It's that new captain. I must get to work on his dreams." said Slubgoeb.

And God said, "*Let there be light,*" and Joan appeared with the power of that first light, blinding the demon for a moment.

"What is this?" he asked.

"I am Joan of Arc, sent here to silence you most foul demon!"

"I know you. You are nothing but an illiterate peasant girl."

Joan drew her sword and pointed it at the demon,

"Blasphemer! You will lose your vile, serpent tongue forever!"

Slubgoeb drew his sword, and they began to joust, producing flashing streams of light with each strike.

"You are no angel! That is why He has cast you down!" said the demon.

"I am a new creation sent to crush you under His heel." replied Joan.

"Those were not saints speaking to you back then. It was I and the others filling your head."

"That will be the last lie to ever leave your unholy mouth, Slubgoeb!"

"You see; you know my name and recognize my voice? Why do you think you were bound to the stake and burned? It was because you were guilty, and you are *a new creation. You should have been*

with us after the ashes but instead, he raised you up to sing with the saints and deceive you into thinking you were saved, because your sin was greater than any other and you received a special judgment. And now here you are, where you belong. Let us dispense with this swordplay."

The demon stepped back from Joan.

"Lay your weapon down with mine and let us embrace."

Slubgoeb raised his hands up and his sword was gone, but Joan remained steadfast, her sword pointed straight.

"Now you surrender, demon, because you know you are already defeated. Your lies fall from my armor like the ashes from my body."

Joan's sword vanished as she raised her arms towards heaven.

"What now little peasant girl, are we going to dance?"

She lowered her arms and moved towards the demon.

He laughed, *"Ha ha ha. So, we* are *going the dance."*

"No. We are not. You will now be silenced."

She was suddenly wrapped in armor as she took a step closer to the demon. He tried to step back but was frozen in place.

"And you will not have the captain."

"He is already dead!" shouted the demon.

"He is already saved," declared Joan.

Joan closed the distance between them and placed her hands around the demon's throat.

"This is not permitted! It is not within the demon accords between heaven and hell. An angel cannot touch a demon! We battle with swords!"

"As you said. I am no angel; and I am no longer a saint. I am a new creation sent to silence the spawn."

The light intensified on Joan's hands, as she placed her right hand over his mouth. It grew in brightness, there was lightning, then the darkness of the belly of the beast, for a moment, before the sun rose over the demon on his knees before Joan with his mouth sewn shut.

"Your time of temptation is done. I don't have to read the words to know the truth. I don't have to show mercy like Christ did when he heard their pleas and sent the demons of Legion into the herd of

swine. You, Slubgoeb, are going into the abyss, where there is no light, and your silence is forever." And the demon was swallowed into the mouth of the pit, as his moans faded in the void.

Chapter Seven

They took Irma every day and she felt herself growing desperate and weak. Time began to fold for her, like sheets of seconds, minutes, hours, days, weeks, months, measured by the snap of her suffering, unfolding her flesh. Usually, the soldiers took her out of the cage and down the hall, but sometimes, when they were drunk, they took her there, in front of her children.

Joan was hovering over Nadja as she prayed. Nadja didn't see her but knew she was there.

"Lord, I pray for your mercy. I pray for my papa's safety and that you end my mama's suffering and pain."

Upon hearing this prayer, Joan had a vision of her own death, that she watched from above. Before they lit the fire with their torches, she felt her spirit pulled from her body with the force of a rushing wind and felt nothing but peace and joy unknown as flesh burned to ash. And Joan prayed, *"Lord, I pray for your mercy. I pray that you end Irma's suffering and pain, as you did for me before you brought me home."*

And God heard these prayers and called upon Michael in response.

"Michael."

"Yes Lord."

"I've allowed you to hear these prayers."

"Yes Lord."

"It is time to move forward in this battle."

"Yes Lord."

"You will give counsel and instruction to Joan, so that she will be prepared."

And in a breath Michael was with Joan.

"Joan, your vision was true."

"Thank you, Lord."

"But this will be different."

"How so?"

"It is not time for Irma to be with us."

"What needs to be done?"

"Her spirit will be free while her body is under siege. She will be able to move in the spiritual realm, to see her children, and be fortified. But unlike you, her soul will remain in her temple, and she will be vulnerable. The enemy will try to occupy her flesh and kill her. You must protect her, while she is out of her body in this heavenly realm."

"The Lord knows I am ready to fight," said Joan.

"I have always been ready."

Irma felt empty as the soldiers took her from her children that day. As with every time before, she hugged them, told them it would be alright, she would be back, and told Nadia to sing to her brother and tell him stories about Joan. But these guards were new to her; they were younger and seemed frightened themselves. Before it began, Irma was seized by a sudden paralysis; she couldn't move or speak, felt a ton of pressure on her chest and heard a loud buzzing in her head. She felt herself falling through the cot, like being caught in a rushing wave, through the cement floor, into darkness. She thought she was dying, then felt the same rushing wave lift her above herself. She was floating near the ceiling, which appeared to be sparkling like the sun dancing on the lake's water. She looked down and saw herself with the guards.

She thought about her children and was there, floating above them as they hugged each other and felt her love. Three low-level demons surrounded Irma's body and the two guards who were with her. They had bodies like monkeys with spiderlike arms and legs and pulsated with a red glowing color. One was hanging over

Irma's head. Another was draped over the body of the guard on top of her and the third was standing alongside the second guard, with an arm around his shoulder, whispering into his ear. Then the room was filled with the original light. The demons were stunned by Joan's presence, fully armored, but for her head, and bearing her double-edged sword. One side of the blade was scripted with *The Word of God;* on the other side was written *The Blood of the Lamb.* The demons fell to their knees and cried out in some ancient tongue. Their words brought forth a foul smell which reminded Joan of the cattle dung she shoveled out of the stables as a child.

She raised her sword above her head and said, *"By the blood of the lamb, I vanquish you to the abyss!"* as she swung her sword horizontally through the demons, who became like vapors carried away by a rushing wind that passed through the room.

The guard stopped, and her spirit was pulled back to her body, as he stepped away. The two men looked at each other, speechless, and began to help Irma with her clothes. They couldn't look her in the eyes, but she could see tears welling up in their eyes. They quietly escorted her back to her cell, where she found Nadja sitting with her brother, telling him stories about her Joan of Arc. She sat with them and listened to Nadja light up as she described Joan leading the French army into battle.

Chapter Eight

Irma never saw the two guards again, but overheard others talking about how they had been shunned and beaten for refusing to participate in further rapes. She was no longer afraid. When they came for her, she went easily as she and her children had found a special peace in the heart of their storm. And she had learned much over the passing months. She became familiar with the physical transition of her spirit leaving her body and through that understanding learned to relax and focus on the thought of her children, which would immediately bring her to them. This took some time to master, and she saw many things along the way. She saw the red demon spider monkeys. There was always at least one, sometimes more, depending on who was in the cell. They would emerge from a dark mist and whisper in the guards' ears. Most importantly, she saw the blinding light fill the room each time and felt a great wind propelling her to her children.

To the rapists, Irma became like a corpse, and they began to come for her less often. It frightened them when she would suddenly open her eyes after the rapes, unaffected. Rumors spread that she was a witch. When she hovered above her children, she saw that Nadja was no longer singing to Danir and telling him stories about Joan. Instead, she was praying. She couldn't know that Joan had come to Nadja in a dream.

They were sitting together on a patch of green grass alongside the summer lake lined with wild flowers and reeds. The sun was warm and bright and there were three hummingbirds playfully darting by, making Nadja laugh. They stretched out on the grass and watched. "I love hummingbirds" she said.

"I love them too," said Joan,

"They are amongst my favorites of his creations."

Nadja continued to watch the birds and giggle as they hummed around her head.

"Nadja, look at me."

She turned to Joan.

"Listen to what I have to say. Things are about to change for you and your family and you must understand the power God has given you. You must pray without ceasing."

"How can I do that? I have to sleep and eat. . ."

"My child I learned when I was in this world, that it doesn't mean praying out loud or in your mind without end, but being always mindful of Our Lord in everything we do and all that we say, thanking him continuously for each breath and step we take."

"I think I understand," said Nadja.

"You will learn," said Joan, "and understand more, as you practice."

"Practice?" asked Nadja.

"Yes. Where people blaspheme his name, you will say 'Good Lord,' in response to your circumstances. When you breathe in deeply, the cleansing breath of the Holy Spirit, you will say 'Thank you, Lord.' You will eventually do this without thinking."

"How is that possible?"

"He lives in your heart. He is with you always. It means you need not fear the enemy. The enemy thrives on our fear, uses it as a weapon against us. But God did not give us a spirit of fear, but a spirit of power, of love, and a sound mind."

"I have the power?"

"Yes, Nadja! All you have to do is pray without ceasing and when you call upon the name of Jesus the enemy has to flee!"

"Amen!" said Nadja.

"Hallelujah!" replied Joan.

"And there's more to know." Said Joan.

"Please tell me."

"There are enough lessons to last a lifetime. We are always learning to grow closer to the Lord. For now, know that God says when two or more gather in my name, there I am in the midst of them."

"Danir," said Nadja, almost in whisper.

"You already know," replied Joan.

"I must teach Danir to pray."

"Amen," said Joan.

When Nadja was awoken by the sound of guards entering the cage, she remembered her dream, like she had just left the cinema after seeing a movie. After they took her mother, she took both her brother's hands as they sat together on the bed and said, "Danir, today I'm going to teach you about Jesus and teach you how to pray."

Chapter Nine

They were again together on their patch of green grass alongside the lake lined with wildflowers and reeds. The sun was setting; the three hummingbirds were playfully buzzing around them, and large multi-colored goldfish were swimming in circles along the bank. This was the place they always met in Nadja's dreams, and sometimes there was a lion and a lamb resting nearby. She had fallen asleep in her dream after a long lesson about the gifts of the Holy Spirit. In her dream she was dreaming of these blue knights that had come to save them. Then Joan began to stroke her hair.

"Nadja. It's time to wake up my precious child. You must go now. It's time to go."

In between dreams and her waking self, Nadja said, "No. the blue knights are here to save us."

Irma continued to stroke her daughter's hair.

"Nadja. Wake up my dear. We are leaving this place. We've been saved."

Nadja opened her eyes and saw her mother and her brother.

"Have we been saved by the blue knights, mama?"

Before Irma could respond, a man entered their cell, wearing camouflage fatigues and a sky blue helmet with the letters UN printed in black on the front.

"Ma'am, you need to get ready. The buses to Croatia will be leaving within the hour."

Irma turned, embraced her children, and whispered to them, "Yes, yes, yes we have been saved by the blue knights."

"But what about papa? How will he be able to find us?" asked Nadja.

"I don't know my love, but we have to go."

Then they were up and moving fast, like they used to move before they were captured, always running, looking for food and water, and running back to the basement when the sirens sounded. Nadja wasn't sure whether she was awake or still dreaming.

They left the cell and ran out of the building. It was still dark, and she looked up to see the if stars were still there. She hadn't seen them since they arrived at the camp. There were blue knights everywhere, directing the women and children to the fleet of buses waiting for them. Some of the women walked slowly, with their shoulders slumped forward and their heads hanging down. Some were alone and others had children. As they passed by, Nadja noticed that the slumping women had sad, sunken eyes; while other women and children ran to the buses. Some were crying and others were laughing. As they approached the buses one of the blue knights ushered them into a large white bus. Nadja thought it was the biggest bus she had ever seen. They entered the vehicle and found an empty row of seats at the very front. The door closed behind them and the blue knight driving the bus started the engine. Nadja looked behind her and saw the same mix of women and children. Some sat silently, mothers and children alike, and stared as if they were seeing nothing. Others were laughing and crying and hugging each other; some couldn't sit still and were dancing in the aisle.

"Nadja. Sit down and don't stare. You know it's not polite," said Irma.

Another blue knight entered the bus with a crate containing brown paper bags. He looked young to Nadja, tall, with blue eyes and tufts of blonde hair sticking out from under his helmet. She had seen boys and very old men at the camp but hadn't seen a young adult since they went into the basement. He spoke their language but very slowly and with a strange accent.

"Please listen before we take off. We are taking you to refugee relief centers in Croatia where you will stay until you are designated to more permanent facilities. It is usually a six and a half hour drive but may take longer depending on the conditions of the road. We know it is very early and have some sandwiches and water for you that I will now hand out. Please take your seats."

The blue knight handed Irma a bag of food for her family and proceeded to give out all the bags. When he was finished, he returned to the front of the bus and sat down behind the driver directly across the aisle from Nadja and her family. The engine started and the bus moved into a row of several other buses heading out from the camp. The bag contained sandwiches of soft white bread enclosing ham, lettuce, and tomatoes. Irma handed them to her children and watched as they ate ravenously prompting her to caution them to "eat slowly my loves and savor each bite as a blessing."

Nadja didn't know if she was in a dream, in a dream, in a dream. Her mother had placed Danir down on the seat between them but still had her arm across Nadja's shoulders. Danir had fallen asleep. When Irma looked at her, Nadja didn't see her mother as she had been since everything had changed. She didn't see the smiley twinkle she used to see when her mother would tickle her. But she also didn't see as much fear as before. Irma leaned closer to Nadja, who could feel her breath on her cheek.

"You should get some sleep."

"I'm not tired Mama."

"Okay, but let's try to sleep for a while," said Irma as she pulled Nadja closer to her so her head was on her shoulder and positioned Danir so he was lying across their laps.

But she couldn't sleep like most of the women and children on the bus. She had never been driven farther than the cabin on the lake, which took less than an hour. She was sitting next to the window and stared out almost the entire ride. The small villages she knew from trips to the cabin were all gone, but for traces of the houses and buildings that once stood. The land in between these places was scarred by blackened fields, naked trees and dotted with craters of various sizes that Nadja knew were caused by the bombs. She felt a darkness in her heart seeing this destruction, that made her angry enough to scream. The bus stopped a few times so people could go to the bathroom, but when it was moving, Nadja looked out the window, hour after hour. The constant growling of the engine and the slight rumbling one could feel from the movement seemed to cover them in a blanket of calm. And outside the window, everything started to look the same to Nadja, like the cartoons she used to watch where she could see that the bear kept running past the same trees. And just as she started to think they were driving in a huge circle, she fell asleep.

She was back in the cage searching frantically for her book. It wasn't under her jacket pillow where she always kept it. It wasn't wrapped in the blanket or under the bed. She couldn't find it anywhere! But it had to be there! There was a blue knight in the cage with her speaking softly, "We must go young lady. The buses are leaving."

"No! I can't leave without my book!"

He tried to place his hand on Nadja's shoulder, but she evaded him by scrambling around the room looking for her book.

"We can find you another book when we get to Croatia."

"No! There is no other book!"

Then she heard her mother's voice.

"Nadja. Wake up. We are here."

Nadja suddenly became paralyzed and could not speak."

"Nadja. Wake up my dear. We must go now."

The cage slowly filled with light as Nadja struggled to open her eyes but her eyelids felt so heavy.

She was looking in her mother's whispering eyes.

"You've been sleeping for hours."

"Mama, I left my book behind."

"Oh Nadja, we can find you another book."

Tears streamed down Nadja's cheeks.

"There is no other book."

Chapter Ten

She felt empty, like her stomach when she was hungry only this was in her heart. The pain was constant and there was no relief like the food that filled her. She had never been apart from her book since she found it. It had been three and a half years since the war started. Nadja was now 11 years old. The new camp was nice. They stayed in a dormitory with other families. Nadja and Danir slept in a bunkbed and their mom had her own bed right next to them. She took top bunk and teased Danir that he was too small for the top, although he was now almost as tall as her, but still very thin. They both were. They had three warm meals a day, fresh sheets, new clothing and access to showers and hot water. They felt safe for the first time since the start of the war. When Nadja and Irma looked at each other with their whispering eyes, Nadja saw that almost all the fear was gone.

The blue knights were a constant presence. But Nadja wasn't sleeping well. She often had the same dream. They were back in the cage, and she couldn't find her book, but Joan was not there to help. She started to believe it was because she lost the book and became very sad. They were safe now, so she stopped praying. She forgot about the dream lesson of praying without ceasing. Danir didn't want to pray with her anyway. He was too busy running around and playing with his new friends. Nadja didn't want to make friends.

Irma didn't seem to notice. She was busy with the other mothers, talking all the time, and meeting with the blue knights. Nadja thought often about the basement, where she found the book, the cage, the guards and her mother. She started to dream about when the guards would come and take her mama away and sometimes wake up in the middle of the night.

Irma wasn't ignoring her children. She was with them for every meal and made sure they were tucked in safely each night. There were some programs for the children but mostly they were free to run around and play. Danir seemed fine but she noticed that Nadja kept mostly to herself.

The first couple of weeks the UN staff kept busy conducting medical examinations and providing care and medical treatment when needed. A great concern among the women was pregnancy. Irma knew some of the families from Sarajevo and tried to comfort those who were found to be pregnant. She simply breathed a deep sigh of relief when she found out she was not. They were told that the housing was temporary and that arrangements were being made for a massive move of refugees to other Western European countries. They were advised that it could happen at any time, so a constant cloud of uncertainty hovered above.

Irma couldn't begin to process what had happened. She could only hold on to the tangible fragments of her sanity, her children, until she knew they were safe.

They were back in the basement sitting around the fire. Danir was sleeping and Nadja watched as Irma placed the books on the fire; she clutched her book of Joan closer to her chest with her right arm and saw the cover and pages of the books start to curl up as black smoke filled the space. She smelled the burning paper, which was like the wood they burned but different with a subtle chemical odor. Irma turned towards Nadja and stared, not with her whispering eyes, but a strange, angry look.

"Nadja, give me that book."

Nadja crossed her arms and pressed her book closer to her heart. She shook her head back and forth.

"Nadja! Give me that book!"

"No mama. Please let me keep it. It's the only thing I have left."

"Nadja. We talked about this. There is no God and these books are dangerous."

"But you said I could keep it."

Irma suddenly grabbed Nadja's right hand.

"Nadja, my sweet. We talked about this, and I told you we had to burn these books so we could be safe."

Nadja resisted her mother's force and started to lean in the opposite direction.

"No Mama, please let me keep it."

Irma lost her patience, grabbed both of Nadja's arms with her own two hands and pulled them apart releasing the book to Nadja's lap. She quickly snatched it up and tossed it into the fire.

"No!" screamed Nadja as she reached for the book, which was already starting to burn.

"Nadja!" yelled Irma as she grabbed her daughter and pulled her to her chest.

Nadja continued to struggle to get free.

"Nadja, Nadja please stop, please Nadja just stop."

"Nadja, wake up my dear, wake up now."

Nadja startled awake and found herself in her mother's arms.

"Are you okay my sweet girl? You were screaming in your sleep."

Nadja felt out breath and couldn't speak. She was exhausted. The dream was playing in her head, like another movie, and they had just walked out the theatre. She thought for a moment that she could feel the heat on her hands from the fire.

"Nadja. I told you we had to be ready, always ready to move. Danir is already up. It's time for us to go." And they were up and moving again.

Chapter Eleven

There was a buzz of activity in the dormitory. All the lights were on and Nadja saw dozens of Red Cross workers wearing their white jackets with a large red cross on the back and smaller crosses on the front. They were hurriedly moving around the space encouraging the women and children to get up, use the bathrooms, and head out of the building. There was a tall Red Cross woman at the front of the dorm speaking into a megaphone.

"Only bring what you can carry! Everything will be provided when we reach our destination. Please move in an orderly fashion. There are buses waiting outside with plenty of room for everyone."

Nadja was still exhausted from her nightmare. Her mother took her and Danir by their hands and began to lead them towards the exit. Nadja suddenly remembered the explosions that blew them down when they left Sarajevo and were heading for the Red Cross camp and pulled back from her mother's grip.

"Nadja. What are you doing? We must go, now. We've been waiting for this."

Nadja tried to catch her breath. She thought she could hear the fighter jets and the bombs and could feel the heat from the blasts and bursting light.

"Mama what about the bombs? There were bombs when we left for the Red Cross. Are they taking us to the Red Cross camp? And what about papa. How is he going to find us?!"

Nadja felt short of breath and Danir began to cry. Irma kneeled and put her arms around her crying children while others rushed past them. She knew that after all that had happened, even if her husband survived, it was not likely they would see him again. He still followed the Quran and her being the victim of numerous rapes left her unholy in his eyes. She spoke softly, "Oh, my darlings. We are safe now. The war is over. There are no more bombs, and we are going to a better place. We have been waiting for this. And I don't know about your papa. I don't know if we'll see him again."

Irma continued to hug her children until she felt their fear subside. She pulled back and looked at them with her whispering eyes and asked, "Are you ready?" They nodded together and were up and out the door.

It was dark outside, but Nadja could see a caravan of six white buses against the shadows of the large mountains that surrounded the camp. It had been a cold winter, and she could see everyone's breath, and the exhaust coming from the pipes at the back of the buses as the low rumbling of the engines permeated the darkness. There were lines forming at each bus and a Red Cross woman directed them to the last bus in line. The mothers were looking straight ahead but the children, like Nadia, were seeing each other, with the same questioning eyes. This time they were first to get on and found a seat at the back of the bus. Danir had stopped crying and was resting in Irma's arms. Nadja watched as the bus filled up. Other than a few sleepy, cranky children there was a blanket of quiet covering them all.

Nadja had taken her place alongside the window and was determined to stay awake during this trip. She kept her eyes on the dark shadow mountains that took on more shape and detail as the sun began to rise. Unlike their trip from Sarajevo to Croatia, where the scarred land passed by like a movie of destruction replaying the same wasteland over and over, Nadja marveled as the buses drove through a landscape of huge mountains on one side and the sea on the other. She was about to meet her second saint, a tour guide who would create a little magic for the trip.

Nadja would learn that Joanna was a graduate student studying Geography and Geoinformatics at the University of Copenhagen when the war started. As an undergrad, she majored in Western European History and Architecture. She stood five feet, ten inches tall, had blonde hair, hazel eyes and a prominent jaw framing a dimpled chin. She was an avid hiker and rock climber, resulting in a well-muscled body. After the Srebrenica Massacre, at the age of 22, she decided to leave school and become a Red Cross volunteer. She had been at the Red Cross station outside of Sarajevo when it was bombed and 60 people died. She was now 25 and her family was relieved that the war had ended, and she was working in the transportation and care of Bosnian refugees heading to the Netherlands.

She quickly noticed the girl in the back of the bus. She had a very light complexion with dark brown eyes, auburn hair and appeared to be 10 or 11 years old. Most of the passengers were sleeping or simply resting, quietly. Joanna knew they had been through a lot, things unimaginable, and they had waited for months for this transport, without any certainty of their future, of when, or where they would be going. But this little girl had been staring out the side window the entire time, sometimes turning to look out of the back of the bus, as if she was trying to see everything. She slowly made her way back to Nadja's seat. Irma and Danir were sleeping and Nadja was staring out the side window, completely unaware of Joanna's presence. They were still in Croatia but were passing through the high point of the Dinaric Alps which run parallel to the Adriatic Coast. Joanna noticed the girl was seeing Mount Dinara, one of the most prominent peaks of the range. Winter was receding to spring, and the green mountain peaks were capped with snow.

"You're looking at Mount Dinara," said Joanna, It remains snowcapped most of the year."

Nadja turned in her seat, slightly startled, then turned back to look out the window.

"It's beautiful," she said. "The bombs did not fall here."

"No. The bombs did not reach this far. I'm Joanna. What is your name?"

"Nadja."

Joanna looked at Irma and Danir sleeping, with his head on her lap.

"And this is your mother and brother?"

"Yes. His name is Danir."

"Well, Nadja. It is my pleasure to make your acquaintance."

"Thank you, ma'am."

"Please, call me Joanna. And I am happy to be on this trip with you and your family."

Irma groaned a bit, shifted her position on the seat, woke up with a start and stared at Joanna.

"Hello ma'am. I didn't mean to disturb you. Can I get you anything? All is well. I was just talking with your daughter about the beauty of the Dinaric Alps. I'm Joanna."

Irma looked at Nadja and could tell she was eager to continue talking with Joanna.

"How do you do, Joanna. Irma. I'm fine right now. Thank you for asking. Nadja's not bothering you, is she?"

"Oh no, no bother at all. I've always loved the mountains and everything in between. She seems fascinated by the land and I'm happy to share what I know."

"Okay. Maybe all this knowledge she's about to receive will tire her out and she can take a nap. How long is the trip?"

"Thirteen hours, depending on the weather conditions."

"Okay. Just don't let Nadja take up all your time. I know you have other responsibilities."

"My main responsibilities are to make everyone comfortable and answer any questions."

Joanna looked back at the rest of the passengers.

"Right now, everyone seems to be resting comfortably, and I think Nadja may have a few questions."

Nadja nodded and turned her attention back to the scene outside the window.

"Thank you, Joanna," said Irma as she leaned back with her nestling boy and closed her eyes. Joanna turned back to Nadja and noticed the scene outside had gradually changed, signaling that they were approaching the border getting closer to the Balkan Peninsula. They were now seeing the extensive rock formations leading to the plains north from the Balkans.

"That's about 500 feet of limestone you're looking at Nadja, but it's still part of the Alps."

"There are different kinds of stones?" asked Nadja.

"Yes, many," said Joanna.

Thus began the Q&A session that lasted the rest of the journey.

For the next dozen hours, Joanna was in Geography heaven explaining to Nadia, as they moved from the Balkans, how the terrain changes into the lowlands of the Pannonian Basin, which cover large parts of Hungary and extend from northern Croatia. She marveled with her at the contrast of this area of flat plains. As they passed through Austria and Slovenia, Joanna told her how the Alps continued through Europe, offering additional majestic views. She also told Nadja about the Danube River Basin, how the Sava and Drava rivers in Croatia are tributaries of the Danube, and they would be following the broader Danube basin through parts of Hungary and Austria. She wanted Nadja to see how everything was connected.

"You see Nadja, it's all part of God's glory in nature, and being part of it, feeling that peace and

grace . . ."

"Is like praying without ceasing." Nadja finished Joanna's sentence for her.

"Yes," added Joanna, with a sense of awe, "That's it, like praying without ceasing."

Once they started moving through central Germany, Joanna tried to identify as many trees as she could as they passed through a mix of forests, hills, and plains. She explained to Nadja how the countryside is characterized by a mix of agricultural land and wooded areas.

Their journey eventually followed the path of the Rhine River, northwest toward the Netherlands, again shifting the landscape dramatically to an artificially created land of flat terrain.

Joan and Michael kept watch over the entire trip.

"It is wonderful that Nadja has met Joanna," said Michael.

"Yes," agreed Joan, "The Lord is using Joanna to unveil God's great glory in nature, thereby increasing her faith."

"And bringing her closer to him," added Michael, "All part of His plan."

The time passed quickly, and Joanna rejoiced in her new friend, an aspiring geographer. And Nadja was refreshed by all she had seen and learned. She stayed awake the entire time and thought of nothing but the mountains, the rivers, the forests and the plains. They had arrived and were moving again, off the bus and into the red-brick King Willem I Barracks in Copenhagen, Denmark.

Chapter Twelve

The Red Army Barracks were originally built in the 1890s for the Guard Hussars of the Royal Danish Army. The pentagonal fortress consisted of sixteen buildings with a capacity for 700 residents. Additional buildings had been constructed, bringing the total capacity to approximately 1000 refugees. There were no men between the ages of 18 and 40 to be found. The caravan of buses from Croatia had arrived carrying approximately 400 passengers. Lines were forming where Red Cross volunteers were handing out clean sheets, pillowcases and towels, along with hygiene items.

Joanna helped each refugee off the bus with a hand and kind words. She knew that Nadja, her mother and brother, would be the last to get off and a place in her heart had opened for her young geography student. As she helped Irma and Danir off the bus Irma turned and said, "Thank you, Joanna, for your time and kindness. You made this into a very special trip for Nadja. You made it so much easier."

"It was my pleasure," she replied. "And thank you for sharing a little about Nadja, like how she lost her book about Joan of Arc. I hope she will enjoy the stories in the New Testament."

"I hope so as well," said Irma.

"Nadja is so smart. She's a wonderful girl and you should be very proud."

"I am. Thank you again. Come Nadja. Say thank you and goodbye to Joanna. We have to get in line."

Nadja stood on the bottom step of the bus and stared at the large, three-story buildings with bright red brick walls and white window and door frames. She had never seen such long buildings. Joanna helped Nadja down and kneeled in front of her, holding her hands.

"Thank you for spending time with me Nadja. It was a joy teaching you about the mountains. You are a very bright student."

Tears began to well up in Nadja as she asked Joanna, "Aren't you staying with us?"

"No. I'm sorry Nadja. I have to return to pick up more families, but I can visit you when I get back."

Nadja reached around Joanna's neck with both arms, and they embraced.

"Nadja, there's something special I need to do for you before I leave."

"What is it?" she asked excitedly.

"Is it okay if I pray for you and your family?"

"Okay," she said.

"Okay then." Joanna replied. "Just a quick prayer before we go. Lord, thank you for your mercy and grace. Thank you for placing Nadja and her family in my life. I lift them up to you now, along with all the other families here, and pray you bless them abundantly with your healing love and give them strength and wisdom as they move forward with their lives."

They released their embrace, held hands, and looked into each other's eyes.

"Amen?" asked Joanna.

"Amen." answered Nadja then added, "And Lord please protect Joanna and bring her back to us soon."

They shared a quick hug, Joanna stood to get back on the bus, and Nadja turned to join her mother and brother who were still standing in line. But she reached out and touched her arm.

"Nadja, wait. I almost forgot. I have a gift for you."

She turned around as Joanna kneeled back down, dug into her jacket pocket, pulled out a small New Testament in a bright orange cover and handed it to her.

"Your mother said it was okay for me to give this to you. It's only The New Testament, not the whole Bible, but that's the really good part."

Nadja looked at the small book in her hand and thought about her book of Joan and how Joan had never read the Bible. She couldn't read but knew what it said.

Nadja looked back at her mother who was standing at the end of one of the many lines, still holding Danir's hand. She turned back to Joanna as they heard her mother call to her.

"Nadja, come now, the line is moving."

She placed the Bible in her coat pocket, hugged Joanna around her neck, gave her a kiss on the cheek, and ran to her mother and Danir.

The Lord summoned the archangel, Michael.

"I know you heard all that was said."

"Yes Lord. She's praying again."

"Of course, Michael, as we knew she would. And she is also now armed with a Bible. Let Joan know. It's time to get back to work. The enemy will be launching a new attack."

The barracks were set up dormitory-style but no bunk beds this time. Everyone had their own bed. The Red Cross was well prepared. The buildings were immaculately clean; there was a fully staffed kitchen crew and a stockpile of donated clothing that had been cleaned and folded. The heat was working, the new residents were already well fed from their first hot meal, freshly showered and most were resting. They had no notion of the plague to come, hundreds of international journalists about to descend upon them in the coming days, weeks, and months.

Ranah Patel was an aspiring journalist working for *The Times*. She was 25 years' old, an only child raised in London by her parents, first generation immigrants from India, and had graduated from the London School of Journalism with high honors. She had gained a lot of attention by her coverage of the Srebrenica Massacre, on which her articles were also picked up by *The New York Times*.

She even thought about writing a book and was starting to believe she could be considered for the Pulitzer Prize through personal interviews with the women who had survived the rape camps run by the Bosnian Serbs in Bosnia and Herzegovina. She also had a college friend who worked as an administrator for the Red Cross. Ranah had gained access to some of the informational records of the refugees and became very interested in Irma Kovacevic, a clinical psychologist who had graduated from the International University of Sarajevo. She imagined what in-depth and insightful interviews she could have with such an intelligent and accomplished woman.

Chapter Thirteen

Glubuse, a smaller version of Slubgoeb, was a demon assigned to the temptation of pride. He had been working on Ranah for quite some time. It began when she was named the valedictorian of her graduating class. He was looking forward to her coverage of the refugee camp. He had been advised of Slubgoeb's failure because of the interference from the so-called saint, the peasant girl Joan. He understood that Slubgoeb had actually been vanquished into the abyss by Joan, in fulfillment of the word that the saints would do greater things than the son! This had caused some concern within the regiment but the girl, Nadja, had stopped praying and rape was no longer a priority. She had uttered a simple prayer upon arrival at The Red Barracks, but it was assessed as more of a mental expression of gratitude, rather than a call from the heart. There was the matter of the pocket-sized New Testament she had been given but through the oppression of depression and targeted nightmares, it could easily be lost.

The hoard of journalists had fallen upon the refugees like a plagued. Some of the refugees talked animatedly with the visitors. Others sat and stared. Most seemed bewildered by all the attention. It was a daily event, and it appeared that most reporters were attempting to conduct as many interviews as possible. Ranah had a different plan. She just wanted to tell one story, Irma's story.

It was several months before Ranah was able to visit the Red Barracks. During this time, Irma had been counseling many women. It had always been her practice of self-care. But this time, it was a way of escaping her own trauma. She had never experienced such fear and facing it was terrifying. It was like a dream to her, a nightmare she locked away in her mind, lest she lose it. She stayed focused on her children and the women she could help. It started with those she knew from Sarajevo, who knew about her background and felt safe to approach her. Then word spread, and she eventually started running small groups.

Nadja had been reading her Bible and memorizing her favorite verses. She was mesmerized by the stories of the miracles Jesus performed but deeply saddened by how he suffered on the cross. She and Danir had adjusted to their lives at the Barracks. Danir spent most of his time playing soccer with the boys. Nadja continued to stay mostly to herself, but there were organized outings like swimming and trips to nearby parks she was able to enjoy.

When Ranah arrived, she was briefed by some of the journalists she was friendly with. She knew it would be a delicate process. Some of the women were unreachable and most of the reporters did not want to re-traumatize the rape victims. Some didn't care; they wanted the gruesome details in order to tell the world what had happened in Bosnia.

When Ranah heard about the woman who counseled others she knew it was Irma. She wasn't hard to find. As Ranah made her way through the grounds and barracks that first day, she saw a group of several women sitting together in a tight circle, with one leading a discussion. It was a beautiful fall day, and they had arranged some chairs on a grassy courtyard surrounded by the red barracks. She tried not to be too obvious as she slowly approached to try and listen in. They were discussing the men lost from their lives when Irma noticed the eyes averted from the circle. This would happen when intruding journalists approached, and most had learned to stay away when a group was engaged.

Irma turned to find a beautiful young Indian woman with dark brown skin, long black hair tied in a ponytail, and large expressive green eyes that caught Irma's glance. She had a leather briefcase strapped across her shoulder and was standing a few feet away.

"Can I help you?" asked Irma.

"Oh, I'm sorry. I didn't mean to interrupt. This is my first day here. I'm Ranah Patel and I'm a journalist with *The Times* in London."

"That's very nice Ms. Patel, but this meeting is not open to journalists."

"Of course. Please forgive me for intruding. I'm just trying to get my bearings around here."

"I'm sure you'll find your way." said Irma, as she turned back to the group.

Ranah stepped away and found a picnic table across the courtyard. It was late in the day as she sat down, took out her notebook and began writing. She observed the activity around her, mostly boys kicking around a soccer ball and a group of girls playing volleyball, but she focused primarily on the group of women she had just encountered. There was a process in place. One would speak at a time, leading to a round of responses. There was laughter, tears, and silence. Ranah watched the women for an hour until the group broke up with hugs and kisses. Ranah waited until Irma was alone before approaching her.

"Excuse me. I just want to apologize again for interrupting your meeting."

Ranah held out her hand.

"Ranah Patel. It's my first day here."

"You said that before," replied Irma as she reached out and firmly shook Ranah's hand.

"Irma Kovacevic. No worries. You'll find your way. Just take your time and be careful. Try to just listen to anyone who wants to talk."

"I will do that. Thank you and I hope to see you again."

"Have a good night Ms. Patel."

As Ranah sat on the bus taking her back to the hotel she was staying at in downtown Copenhagen, she was excited about the possibilities of spending time with Irma Kovacevic. *This is perfect, she thought. She's actually running support groups with some of the women.*

Chapter Fourteen

Nadja started each day the same. The first thing she did after getting up in the morning was to read a chapter from her Bible. She felt obligated to Joanna since it was a gift and hoped to see her again and tell her about her favorite stories and verses. Today she was reading from 1 Thessalonians chapter 5.

When she came to verse 17, "pray without ceasing," she paused as the sun peeked through the window illuminated just those words. And she remembered a dream about Joan in which she told her what it meant to be mindful of God's presence. And her heart was broken. She had prayed when they were in the camp and God had answered her prayers as they had been rescued and were now safe. But she didn't know what was real or a dream and when she lost her book of Joan, she lost her connection.

The book was gone, left behind in that terrible place they never spoke about, that place she tried not to think about. She looked around the dormitory. There were a few people in the bathroom across from her and everyone else was at breakfast. She felt her heart pounding and started beathing deeply. Then she just prayed, softly, almost in a whisper

"Dear God. Please forgive me for not praying and thank you for keeping us safe. Please bless my mother and brother, and all the other families here and be with Joanna and please Lord, I pray we can see her again."

And The Lord called to Michael.

"Again, you have been permitted to hear these prayers."

"Yes Lord! As always, your timing is perfect."

"Call upon Joan and tell her to prepare for battle with Glubuse tomorrow. And as a special gift, you can release some of the secret things from her life on earth."

"Thank you, Lord. I will do as you say."

And Michael called to Joan.

"I know you heard Nadja's prayers," he said.

"Oh yes!" replied Joan. "Thank the Lord, she is praying again!"

"He continues to do a new thing in you Joan, allowing you to hear these prayers. And tomorrow you will engage in battle once again, this time with Glubuse, a foul demon who oversees the sin of pride. He has been working on a journalist, Ranah, who is starting to care more about herself, than anyone else, regardless of whom she may hurt in her pursuit of the story. Right now, she has focused all her attention on Irma."

"The Lord knows I am prepared for battle!" declared Joan.

"He does and he wants to equip you with more power this day."

"But I already have all I need."

"You do Joan, but this gift of knowledge will bring you peace and Grace."

"Then I am blessed to receive it and will rejoice in his name."

"Joan, you know His Word says that the secret things belong to him, but the things revealed belong to us forever."

"I know it is His Word."

"In your life in the flesh you heard the voices of the saints, Catherine and Margaret."

"I did. They told me what to do and gave me what I needed."

"Yes, and it was one of the things that your accusers used to convict you as a heretic, arguing before the corrupt church and heads of state, that you were in league with Satan and the voices were from demons. And when you were in chains, facing the fire, you had doubts."

"And I am still ashamed."

"No! Let that go! You acted no differently than Our Lord in the garden when he asked the father to take away the cup of death.

The voices were true, and you heard from the saints Catherine and Margaret as a prophetic vision of your own voice to be heard today.! Go now. The moment is upon us, the battle has begun."

Ranah arrived at the barracks in the afternoon around the same time as the previous day hoping to find Irma in the same place with her ladies. Her career was already flourishing, and she could almost taste the Pulitzer Prize. Her hope was rewarded. She sat at the picnic table where she was the day before and started thinking about how she would approach Irma after the group ended.

Glubuse went right to work.

"This will be amazing. What an opportunity. You can tell her that her story will reach so many women around the world, who have suffered from war."

And Ranah thought *I have to tap into her core purpose as a therapist and help her to see how many women she could help. We could write a book together.*

"Yes," said Glubuse, "which could win you The Pulitzer Prize and be made into a movie."

The group ended with the same ceremony and Ranah walked across the courtyard to meet Irma.

She waved as she approached.

"Hi Irma, do you have some time to talk with me?"

Irma stopped to wait for Ranah, so as not be chased down, as these reporters were quick to do.

"Hi Ranah?"

"Yes. You remembered. Do you have time to talk with me about the work you are doing here?"

"I'm not sure what work you're talking about."

Glubuse stood ready in the spiritual realm with the script he had prepared, when he was momentarily blinded by the original light of creation. As his sight returned, he beheld Joan, before him, wearing her armor and bearing her doubled edged sword.

He groaned, "Damnation! I know who you are and they told me that your charge was done through the vanquishing of Slubgoeb. This is not rape, only pride, and that is outside your jurisdiction."

"And I know you foul Glubuse; and my jurisdiction is where God sends me!"

And Ranah made a quick decision to go all out.

"Irma, when I arrived yesterday my colleagues told me about the special woman who was counseling the others, and I did my homework."

"What did you learn?"

"You graduated from the International University of Sarajevo, where you were valedictorian, and you are a respected and well-known therapist."

"Those things are true;" replied Irma, "but what does it have to do with anything that's happening here?"

Joan and Glubuse had squared off, the demon brandishing a dark blade, pale in size and shape compared to Joan's sword. They began to battle but, with each clash of the blades, Glubuse stepped back and began to whine.

"This is against The Demon Accords! Saints are not permitted fight with demons!"

"As I told your wretched brother, Slubgoeb, I am no longer a saint, and I am no angel. I am a new creation and not subject to your demon accords which are not binding on the host of heaven. They are a lie your fallen lord spoke into your mind to get you to do his bidding."

"But what you are doing here is amazing Irma."

"All we are doing here is surviving, together."

"But if we could share the details of the stories, of your own story, to capture the depth of your experience and document how far you've come, along with the women you have helped."

Glubuse continued to back away from Joan and was down to one knee, as she raised her sword high above her head.

"No matter how many stories could be told, no one, none of your readers, could ever understand what we have been through."

"Of course, Irma, of course, but rape, mass rape, has been the ugly underbelly of war throughout history, and. . ."

"Ranah, have you ever been raped?"

Glubuse was down on both knees pleading for mercy

"Oh please, holy saint, or angel, or whatever you are, holy one, don't send me into the abyss as you did to Slubgoeb."

"No," answered Ranah "thank God, I have not, I, I, . . ."

"Send me into that flock of crows below that I may fly away; show mercy as your Lord did to Legion when he sent them into the herd of swine," cried Glubuse.

"So, you couldn't know that each time you are raped, it's like a death." said Irma.

"But I don't have to personally experience something to write about it," replied Ranah.

"I could never reach the mercy displayed by my Lord, but you know the swine rushed into the river and drowned. Where do you think Legion went?"

"Perhaps," said Irma, "but what do you ask someone who has suffered multiple deaths?"

"I, I, I don't know," replied Ranah.

"Then, what are you looking for; how often, how long, how many times?"

Ranah looked down at her feet. She felt light in her head, and somewhat queasy.

"Are you looking for a body count, like the rest of your colleagues?"

"Go now into the abyss, foul demon Glubuse!" shouted Joan as she brought her sword down upon the shriveling demon, who's moan echoed into eternity as he descended into the pit.

Ranah had never experienced anything like a revelation before, but as she stood before Irma, she was never more certain about anything in her life.

"Irma. I am so sorry."

Ranah couldn't stop the tears now rushing down her face.

"I am so ashamed."

As is her nature, Irma quickly intervened.

"Ranah, stop. You are obviously a beautiful and intelligent woman, but you are also very young and have much to learn. You are meant to be here and have something to say. My daughter, Nadja, has begun reading the Bible since we arrived. A Red Cross worker gave it to her as a gift. Before the war we could've been arrested in Bosnia for possessing this book, or the Quran, or any religious work. But she likes to quote verses to me that she's memorized. The other day she said something about being quick to listen and slow to speak. Stay here and quietly watch and listen; then write what you see and hear. Volunteer at the nursery and spend time with the casualties of war. You can ask yourself and your readers the questions later."

The two women embraced for a long time; then walked away from each other.

Chapter Fifteen

It was early spring in 1996. Nadja had never heard of the Village of Velp in the Netherlands. It sounded magical to her. *The Kingdom of Velp*. They were excited about having their own home. Irma told her children that there were places offering to help refugee families and the Village of Velp had chosen them to give them a cottage to live in, work for Irma, and a school for Nadja and Danir to attend.

Irma had applied for asylum, and through a combination of resettlement processes, with assistance from the United Nations High Commissioner for Refugees, had secured travel permits for herself and her children. Seeing Joanna again was a wonderment to her and affirmed her hope that they would be okay. And all she could think to tell her children was the people of Velp were waiting to welcome them, and it was time to go.

The sun was just beginning to rise as they left the barracks for the last time. Many families had already gone. Nadja saw there were no huge buses to board, just a few white vans with red crosses, heading in different directions. A couple of families had already boarded the van they were directed to, and they were the last to get on.

Nadja felt tired and wasn't looking forward to another long trip. She had gotten used to the barracks and had even started making friends. She was the last in line and stood staring at her feet when she heard a familiar voice.

"Excuse me young lady."

She looked up but couldn't see the driver clearly, as the sun was just cresting the tree ridge and was caught in her eyes. She raised her hand to shield the sun and saw,

"Joanna!"

"Hello Nadja. Are you taking the trip to Velp with us? You know it's a nine-hour drive, so we really must get started if we want to make it by sundown."

And all she could say was "Joanna."

Once again, God had answered her prayers and all her doubts about this trip vanished. Seeing Nadja at a loss for words and motion, and wanting to get started on the long drive, Joanna added, "And, not only is this a trip to your new home, it is also a Geography field trip, you will be my copilot and kindly take this seat behind your driver and instructor."

Nadja could barely feel her feet as she stepped up into the van and saw her mother's smiling face and before she took her seat behind her friend, she said, "Joanna!" for the third time, they embraced and were off.

The trip was not long enough for Nadja, as Joanna described everything with joy for all her passengers. The first leg from Copenhagen to the Netherlands was by ferry to Oslo. Joanna called out the views of the Kattegat strait and the Oslofjord with its rough waters and focus on the open sea and the approaching Norwegian coastline.

As they drove off the ferry onto Norwegian soil, she prepared her audience for the dramatic landscape transformations ahead. They initially drove through some rolling hills which soon gave way to the high mountains, deep valleys, dramatic, deep fjords, and narrow inlets of the sea surrounded by steep cliffs.

Joanna could only estimate how many feet above sea level they were as they ascended and descended, following the contours of the land, with ongoing views of valleys and forests. And she couldn't hide her enthusiasm as she drove into the more rugged, higher-elevation terrain, signaling their final approach to Velp.

There were two stops before Velp, where the other families were dropped off. Joanna told her final passengers that there were about 18,000 people living in Velp. It had been a long day, the sun was setting, and she thought she might have taken her lessons a bit too far when she began to explain how Velp became a Catholic enclave within the Dutch Republic in 1631, but was conquered by France in 1794 and sold to the Batavian Republic in 1800.

She was about to discuss the blended architecture of the village when Nadja and her family were spared by the van stopping in front of a small cottage in the woods on the outskirts of town. Nadja barely noticed the small group of women there to greet them. Danir was asleep over Irma's shoulder as she stepped out of the van, turned and said, "Joanna, I can't thank you enough. Good luck on finishing your PhD. Too bad we didn't record this trip. It could've served as your dissertation."

"And I could've titled it On the Road to Velp!"

"I hope you stay in touch," said Irma.

"Oh, I plan on it," replied Joanna.

Once again, Nadja struggled to find the words, "Joanna."

She was fighting back the tears.

"Nadja. You are my number one student, and I know where you live."

Irma stood waiting for Nadja, with a sleepy Danir leaning on her leg, both surrounded by a welcoming party of three joyful women from a local church.

"Your mother is waiting."

"I know. Thank you for coming back for us Joanna. I, I love you."

"I love you too Nadja and I will see you again, okay?"

"Okay," said Nadja as she hugged Joanna, kissed her on the cheek and wept as she ran to her mother.

Joanna took a deep breath, started the van and drove away.

The church ladies brought them into the small two-bedroom cottage to find a warm fire burning, reflecting light off the dark wooden floors with flowered carpets. There was a fully stocked refrigerator with warm pastries fresh from the oven sitting on the kitchen table. In the smaller room they found a bunkbed for Nadja and Danir. In the master bedroom was a queen-sized bed with flowered sheets, a bedspread, and covered pillows. After they were sure the family was settled, the women departed with good wishes and advised that they would come by the following day with more supplies and information about Irma's work and the children's school.

Exhausted but at peace, Irma pulled the covers down, laid on her new bed and took in a deep breath. She could hear Nadja and Danir still exploring what was in the refrigerator. She closed her eyes and continued with her cleansing breaths when she noticed the quiet that surrounded her. She opened her eyes to see Nadja and Danir standing in the doorway to her bedroom. She patted the mattress and her children joined her. The three of them first slept together at the prison camp in Sarajevo. Irma pulled up the covers, and they slept together more deeply than ever until the dawn of their new life.

In the realm in-between heaven and earth, Michael and Joan looked down upon the family.

"Look how they sleep together, so peacefully, at long last," said Joan.

"It is a healing sleep," said Michael, "You have done well with this one."

"And I am ready for my next assignment!"

"You will stay with this family, Joan, always, for they will face many trials ahead. but there will be others. We're just getting started. Go now and join your charge in her dream."

Joan and Joanna were sitting alongside Nadja on the green grassy bank along the summer lake, their arms around her shoulders. The sun was shining through the red leaves on the maple trees, sprinkling light sparkles on the water rolling by. They were barefoot, dangling their toes in the water to be tickled by the nibbling goldfish, while the trio of hummingbirds hovered around them.

The End

www.ingramcontent.com/pod-product-compliance
Lightning Source LLC
LaVergne TN
LVHW020657100826
845148LV00012B/2534

* 9 7 8 1 6 6 6 7 8 9 3 7 9 *